To: Doris Stevenson

Thank You
& Enjoy
Reading!

Dr. Catherine J. Johnson
11-18-07

Orpah Walked Ahead of Ruth

Two Faithful Daughters-in-Law of Naomi

by

Dr. Catherine J Johnson

authorHOUSE®

AuthorHouse™
1663 Liberty Drive, Suite 200
Bloomington, IN 47403
www.authorhouse.com
Phone: 1-800-839-8640

© 2007 Dr. Catherine J Johnson. All rights reserved.

No part of this book may be reproduced, stored in a retrieval system, or transmitted by any means without the written permission of the author.

First published by AuthorHouse 9/18/2007

ISBN: 978-1-4343-3115-1 (sc)

Library of Congress Control Number: 2007906842

Printed in the United States of America
Bloomington, Indiana

This book is printed on acid-free paper.

Ruth 1:4-15

4. Now they took wives of the women of Moab: the name of the one was Orpah, and the name of the other Ruth. And they dwelt there about ten years. 5. Then, both Mahlon and Chilion also died; so the woman survived her two sons and her husband. 6. Then she arose with her daughters-in-law that she might return from the country of Moab, for she had heard in the country of Moab that the Lord had visited His people by giving them bread. 7. Therefore she went out from the place where she was, and her two daughters-in-law with her; and they went on the way to return to the land of Judah. 8. And Naomi said to her two daughters-in law, "Go, return each to her mother's house. The Lord deal kindly with you, as you have dealt with the dead and with me. 9. "The Lord grant that you may find rest, each in the house of her husband." So she kissed them, and they lifted up their voices and wept. 10. And they said to her, "Surely we will return with you to your people." 11. But Naomi said, "Turn back, my daughters; why will you go with me? Are there still sons in my womb, that they may be your husbands? 12. "Turn back my daughters, go- for I am too old to have a husband. If I should say I have hope, If I should have a husband tonight and should also bear sons, 13. "Would you wait for them till they were grown? Would you restrain yourselves from having husbands? No, my daughters; for it grieves me very much for your sakes that the hand of the Lord has gone out against me!" 14. Then they lifted up their voices and wept again; and Orpah kissed her mother-in-law, but Ruth clung to her. 15. And, she said, "Look, your sister-in-law has gone back to her people and to her gods.; return after your sister-in-law."

Scripture taken from the New King James Version. Copyright c 1982 by Thomas Nelson, Inc. Used by permission. All rights reserved.

Special Dedication
This book is dedicated to Ashley, Alexis, Honey, Janet, Julie, Kim and to all of my lovely nieces....

Acknowledgements

Thank you, Lucious, Diallo, Ashley and Alexis for your continued love and support. I love you and appreciate you.

Thanks to all of my brothers, sisters, brothers-in-law, sisters-in-law nieces, nephews, and my entire family.

A special "thanks" to Julie for just being you. I love all of you.

To my church family and especially my choir family, I thank you and I love you.

To my friends wherever you may be, I love you and I thank you for your support.

To my co-workers, thank you for all of your support.

Foreword

We find the name Orpah in Ruth 1: verses 4-15 in the Holy Bible (KJV). Although, Ruth, the sister-in-law to Orpah is the significant sister-in-law in this book, oddly enough, Orpah is listed first when discussing the two women. Also, when we read of the two husbands of these women, Orpah's husband Chilion, is mentioned second to his brother, Mahlon, the husband of Ruth. It seems peculiar that these persons are listed in this manner in the Bible. When looking at how the names are placed, it would suggest that Orpah's role was more significant than the role of Ruth. It would appear that the eldest son's wife would be listed first and we would presume that Mahlon is the eldest son since he is listed first whenever the two sons are mentioned. However, Ruth was married to Mahlon and she is repeatedly mentioned after Orpah, who was married to Chilion. Also, it could not be that the names were placed alphabetically, since Mahlon comes after Chilion. Because of how her name is placed ahead of Ruth, we have been sent a message that Orpah was a great woman and Orpah left us a great story. Of course, we do not have the story of Orpah in the Bible like we have the story of Ruth. But, it is the writer's belief that we are to tell her story and this is the author's version of the story of the woman Orpah or as we may say the name today, Oprah's story. When the writer envisions the caravan headed by Naomi, the writer sees Naomi, walking first, Orpah second and Ruth walking behind Naomi and Orpah.

Table of Contents

Acknowledgements ix
Foreword xi
Introduction xv

Chapter One
   Orpah Departs From Naomi and Ruth....................1
Chapter Two
   Orpah Travels Home With Ebenum and Dedum, ..7
Chapter Three
   Orpah Arrives At Her Mother's House 15
Chapter Four
   Orpah Is Back In Her Mother's House 21
Chapter Five
   All Do Not Welcome Orpah Home.......................25
Chapter Six
   Other Worshippers of God 29
Chapter Seven
   Orpah Finds The Other Worshippers of 37
Chapter Eight
   The Worshippers of God Develop 47
Chapter Nine
   They Decide on the Plan..53
Chapter Ten
   The Worshippers Travel To 63
Chapter Eleven
   Sareah Keeps A Secret..69
Chapter Twelve
   God Blessed His Worshippers 79
About the Author...87

Introduction

Names taken from the Bible are of great significance to those who take these names and bestow them upon daughters, granddaughters, nieces, goddaughters and other significant persons in their life. The author speaks of names for females because this book is about a woman in the Bible. It is evidenced through out history that names taken from the Bible have been given to many powerful and famous men and women. Even as I write, new born babies, both male and female, are being named after persons in the Bible. In the majority of the time, these names are taken exactly as they are spelled and pronounced. But, in some cases, the names have been changed for various reasons; however, the similarities can be readily seen and heard. Sometimes, our ancestors changed the spelling or pronunciation to make the name sound more pleasant to the ear, like they did so many other things in life. This is the case, the author believes, that was done to the name of Orpah. It is the author's opinion that our ancestors changed this name to Oprah because it sounded better for a female to be called Oprah rather than Orpah.

We find the name Orpah in Ruth 1: verses 4-15 in the Bible. Although, Ruth, the sister-in-law to Orpah is the significant sister-in-law in this book, oddly enough, Orpah is listed first when discussing the two women. Also, when we read of the two husbands of these women,

Orpah's husband Chilion, is mentioned second to his brother, Mahlon, the husband of Ruth. It seems peculiar that these persons are listed in this manner in the Bible. When looking at how the names are placed, it would suggest that Orpah's role was more significant than the role of Ruth. It would appear that the eldest son's wife would be listed first and we would presume that Mahlon is the eldest son since he is listed first whenever the two sons are mentioned. However, Ruth was married to Mahlon and she is repeatedly mentioned after Orpah, who was married to Chilion. We know, even now, that when listing or saying the names of our children, we usually say the eldest child's name first. Also, it could not be that the names were placed alphabetically, since Mahlon comes after Chilion. We have read that Ruth was the great-grandmother of King David (Matt. 1: 5, KJV) and that Jesus Christ came to us through the line of King David (Matt. 1:16, KJV) and that is very significant, especially to Christians. However, we understand that Ruth was significant, but the Bible is letting us know that the greatness of Orpah should not be overlooked. Because of how her name is placed ahead of Ruth, we have been sent a message that Orpah was a great woman and Orpah left us a great story. Of course, we do not have the story of Orpah in the Bible like we have the story of Ruth. But, it is the writer's belief that we are to tell her story and this is the author's version of the story of the woman Orpah or as we may say the name today, Oprah's story. When the writer envisions the caravan headed by Naomi, the writer sees Naomi, walking first, Orpah second and Ruth walking behind Naomi and Orpah.

In writing the story of Orpah, it is written about her greatness in relationship to the decision to return to her people, the challenges she faced as a single woman who married outside of her people and the manner in which she persevered over difficulties to become a significant woman among her people and among her chosen people; the people of her husband.

When reading this book on the story of Orpah, it is suggested that the reader reads for enjoyment and not factual information. This is one writer's story on the life of Orpah after reading the verses about Naomi, Orpah and Ruth in the Holy Bible (KJV). Some other person may read and write a very different story about Orpah, however, it is the author's belief that this is how Orpah's story will be told to the world. It will be told through those of us who read and write about her. So, read and enjoy the story of this fascinating strong and brave woman called Orpah.

Chapter One

ORPAH DEPARTS FROM NAOMI AND RUTH

I am sure that Naomi knew from the beginning that Orpah would be the one to go back to her people. We can see that Naomi, herself, was a strong magnificent woman who knew that she had to survive on her own and she also knew that she had two beautiful daughters-in-law that she had to protect. Naomi had pondered many nights about her future and the future of her daughters-in-law. They were beautiful and caring young women who had loved her sons with all of their heart. Yet, Naomi knew that God had taken the men in her family for a reason. But, he had let them live with good health to go on with their lives. She was sad, but she had to gather up all her energy for the great task ahead of her. This was not the time for grieving; she had to move on with her life because she knew that this was what God wanted her to do. We can see Naomi with her caravan since she was the head of her household at this point in her life. Naomi walked first behind her trusted servants, Orpah followed Naomi and Ruth followed Orpah with the remaining servants at the tail of the caravan. They had moved out from the country of Moab traveling back to the land of Judah, Bethlehem-judah. Naomi knew well that the land of Judah was her home but not the home of her daughters-in-law. She knew that they would long for their family once leaving the place of their birth and she knew that those in Bethehem-judah would not care for them as they cared for her. Being their primary caretaker, this caused Naomi to worry about the welfare of her daughters-in-law. She loved both of them as she would love her own daughters, but she knew that their mothers were back in the country of Moab.

Naomi sent two of her trusted man servants, Ebenum and Dedum , who had been servants and friends to her sons to bring her daughters-in-law to her tent. When they both arrived, she dismissed Ebenum and Dedum and requested her daughters-in-law to sit with her. She spoke to each of them telling them how they had been good daughters-in-law and how she loves them as she would love her own daughters. She talked about her sons and how they had come to her since their father, Elimelech, had died and asked for her blessings because they wanted to take wives from the women of Moab. She told them that she had cautioned her sons about marrying outside of their kinsmen, but both her sons,

Mahlon and Chilion, preferred them over the women of the people of Judah. Naomi and her daughters-in-law talked throughout the night into the morning when she said to them that they should return back to their mother's house. We see how Orpah and Ruth reacted to Naomi's suggestion. We know that they cried and we know that Naomi, because she loved them so deeply, cried more than her two daughters-in-law. Naomi didn't want them to leave, but she knew that this was the best thing for them because the two of them were still young enough to marry again and have children of their own.

Orpah and Ruth cried and talked about their mother-in-law's suggestion that they each return to their mother's house. I can see Orpah, being the stronger of the two saying to Ruth that Naomi is saying the right thing when she says for us to return home. She tells Ruth that Naomi did not have another son to help her and she will be on her own unless she finds relatives who will take her in and treat her with the respect that she deserves. She goes on to say that if Naomi goes back home with two young single women, certain things may happen to them that are not pleasant because the people in the land of Judah are not their family. She tells Ruth that Naomi will have to find a kinsman who is willing to marry her, since Naomi will most likely not find a husband at her age. This kinsman will have to be willing to purchase the parcel of land that belonged to Elimelech that Naomi will have to sell. When the kinsman buys the land, he is purchasing all that belonged to Elimelech, Mahlon and

Chilion (KJV). She tells Ruth that in Naomi's culture, the nearest kinsman will have to be notified when Naomi advertises the parcel of land and each one will have to decline before the next nearest kinsman can agree or disagree to purchase the land. Orpah goes on to say to Ruth that this could take a long time before she could find a kinsman who will purchase the parcel of land that belonged to Elimelech in Bethlehem-judah. Orpah said to Ruth that if no kinsman is willing to purchase the parcel of land from Naomi, that the two of them may end up living in poverty and Naomi does not want this to happen to her or to her daughters-in-law. Orpah tries to reason with her sister-in-law, but Ruth knows that being with Naomi is far better than what she would have to go back to in the country of Moab. Ruth did not want to go back to the negative comments concerning her marriage and her worshipping the Lord God of Israel. Orpah knew that negative comments would await her too, but she decided to return to her mother's house for Naomi's sake. Ruth told Orpah that she would cling to Naomi and would go with Naomi to Bethlehem-judah and that she would serve Naomi's God. Orpah said that although she would go back to her mother's house, she would no longer serve the gods of her mother, her family and her people. She went on to say that she has found the one and only true God, which is the God of her husband and his people and she would forever serve the God of her husband's people. Orpah also said to Ruth that she knew that God would take her from them

Orpah Walked Ahead of Ruth

and would bring her safely back to her mother's house and would keep her safe as long as she lived. She and Ruth hugged and said that they would forever love each other and that they would some how find the means to stay in touch with each other.

The next morning, after Orpah and Ruth had talked, they went in together to see Naomi. They cried again, but this time, Orpah kissed Naomi and said to Naomi that she would forever be her mother-in-law, but that she was going back to her mother's house in the country of Moab. Somehow, Naomi knew that Orpah would be the one returning to her mother's house. She always knew that Orpah was a more independent person than Ruth and that Orpah would do well on her own. As a mother-in-law, she worried a little more about Ruth and knew that she would have to guide Ruth more than she would have to guide Orpah. However, she felt in her heart that Orpah was going to be just fine and she knew that some day they would see each other again. She also knew that Orpah had spoken with Ruth and she knew that Ruth would always listen and would do as Orpah advised her to do. Naomi now felt much better about taking Ruth back to the land of Judah with her. She knew that Orpah had told Ruth to stay very close to her and she had said to Ruth that our mother-in-law is a very wise woman who knows how to protect you from danger that you cannot see.

Naomi summoned her two loyal servants; Ebenum and Dedum, to come and take Orpah back to her mother's house. She advised them to stay very close to Orpah until she was back with her family. Although she said it loud enough for her trusted servants to hear her say to Ruth that she should leave with Orpah because Orpah was going back to her mother's house and to her gods, Naomi knew in her heart that Orpah would never worship or serve the many gods that her people served and worshipped again. Naomi didn't want to cause her daughter-in-law to have any problems by having anyone think that Orpah was still serving the Lord God of Israel. She said that she was going back to her gods so that the servants accompanying her would not question her when and if they saw her praying to the Lord God of Israel. Naomi and Orpah had talked about how she should carry herself at all times when she returned to her mother's house so that no one would suspect her of serving the God of her husband's family. Naomi advised Ebenum and Dedum to speak to no one but Orpah's mother to let her know that Orpah had decided to come back home while she and Ruth went on to the land of Judah. She entrusted in them a package to be given to Orpah's mother that contained some very important items which belonged to Chilion. She knew that Orpah's mother, like all loving mothers, would know what to do with it and when to give this package to Orpah. Orpah left with Ebenum and Dedum shedding tears while Naomi and Ruth shed tears as they watched her move farther and farther away from them.

Chapter Two

ORPAH TRAVELS HOME WITH EBENUM AND DEDUM,

Orpah had not realized when she was with Naomi and Ruth how far they had traveled from the country of Moab. But once she, Ebenum and Dedum left her mother-in-law's caravan, Orpah knew that her journey back to her mother's house would be a very long and lonely trip. She would not have Ruth with her when she just wanted to talk about their husbands and how much each of them loved their husband. She would not have the sweet voice of Naomi guiding her every move, singing those songs she loved so much and telling her what a wonderful person she was. These thoughts made tears come to Orpah's eyes and they made her heart ache for Naomi and Ruth.

Ebenum was especially close to Chilion and Dedum was closer to Mahlon, but both men had grown up with the sons of Elimelech and Naomi and they loved both of them. Their families had come to the country of Moab with Elimelech and Naomi and they had been loyal servants to the family. They knew that this was the reason; Naomi had called them to accompany her daughter-in-law back to the country of Moab and especially back to her mother's house. Naomi would not give this type of an assignment to just any servant; she had to give it to the ones that she trusted the most. She knew that Ebenum and Dedum would make sure that her daughter-in law returned to her mother's house. They would easily give up their life to protect their friend's wife and the daugther-in-law of their master. Ebenum and Dedum knew that Orpah and Ruth were like Naomi's own daughters. They felt very special having been selected to take Orpah back to her mother's house.

Each night, Ebenum and Dedum would see Orpah praying to their God, the Lord God of Israel. Lord God of Israel is the God of Naomi and Naomi's family in the land of Judah. Orpah had told Ruth and Naomi that she would serve the Lord God of Israel for the rest of her life, because she knew that this was the one and only true God. She knew that her family in the country of Moab did not worship or serve her God, but they worshipped many gods and they would expect Orpah to worship their gods. Orpah knew in her heart that she would never again serve the gods of her mother and her family in her family's compound in the country of Moab. God had brought her through so much and she knew that He was with her even as she traveled back to her mother's house. She did not know what would happen once she got back home, but she knew that things would be all right for her. She had complete faith in God. She had seen how Naomi had gone to God in prayer when her husband and sons had died leaving the women alone. She had seen how Naomi had gathered the strength she needed to make the decision to go back to her people in Bethlehem-judah. Naomi had also said to them that God had given her the strength to make decisions for all of them. Now, Orpah knew that Naomi was not with her to help her gather the strength to move back home and she knew that she really did not want to go back to her mother's house. But Orpah knew that this was what she had to do to make a better life for herself since her husband was dead and she was now on her own.

Ebenum was concerned about Orpah's safety in her mother's house if someone would find out that she was worshipping and serving the God of her husband's family and not their many gods. He had wanted to say something to Orpah about this, but he didn't want to frighten her or to have her upset with him for speaking to her about how and who she should worship and serve. He also feared that she may let Naomi know that he discussed their God with her and Naomi had always been good to him and his family. Ebenum understood his place in Orpah's life and his place was to be a servant to her and to return her to her mother's house with the package that Naomi had entrusted in him and

Dr. Catherine J Johnson

Dedum. But, Ebenum found that with each day and night spent with Orpah on the trip back to her mother's house he was being drawn closer and closer to her. He knew that he could not fall in love with Orpah, but he knew that these feelings were more than just the feelings of a servant and a friend. He knew that he had always liked Orpah in certain ways more than he liked Ruth and now he knew that he was always in love with Orpah. He knew that he could never let her or anyone else know of these feelings. The only person he could talk to about his feelings for Orpah was God and he knew that God would understand. Ebenum knew that God had given him these feelings and he knew that God would make it all right for both of them one day. He had to be patient and wait on God

Orpah found herself on her knees like she had done so many times with Chilion, before his death, and his family. She knew that her mother and her family back in the country of Moab would be watching her to see if she was still serving the God of her husband and they knew that certain postures meant that she was serving the God of her husband's people and not their gods. She also knew that they would watch her eating habits to see what her diet consisted of during the day. Her family would closely watch the activities of the people of the land of Judah living in the country of Moab when they would come out of their territory to an area very close to the family's compound. This is how Chilion and Orpah met and fell in love. She would watch the people of the

Orpah Walked Ahead of Ruth

land of Judah come into their area certain parts of the year for various reasons. It seemed that she and Chilion fell in love instantly and they would say that God blessed their marriage because He sent his family to the country of Moab so that they could meet and marry. Naomi had cautioned her about her manners around her family. Naomi wanted Orpah to continue to serve God, but Naomi wanted Orpah to be careful once she went back to her mother's house. She knew that God would always be with her and He would show her how to behave while in her mother's house. Naomi could remember how Orpah's father had reacted when Orpah and Chilion wanted him to bless their marriage. She knew that he did not welcome Chilion into their family and that he did not want Orpah to marry any person outside of their people. Orpah's mother had been the one who was kind to her son and she loved him as she loved her own sons.

Orpah could see Ebenum walking toward her like he had done so many times before. He would always turn and walk off once he came within so many feet of her. She didn't want Ebenum to walk off this time, so she asked Ebenum how much farther was the country of Moab from them. Ebenum seemed shocked and did not speak, but when she asked him a second time; Dedum spoke up and said that they would have to travel for five more days before they would reach her mother's house. They did not travel at night because the night was for resting and finding food to eat during the day. Dedum had suspected that Ebenum loved Orpah and he wanted to save his friend from embarrassment so he answered for him. Upon seeing the look on Orpah's face once he answered her, he was sure that she, too, loved Ebenum. Dedum did not want this to be since he knew that a servant should not fall in love with his master's daughter or daughter-in-law which was like his own daughter. Also, Chilion had been their trusted friend and Orpah was Chilion's wife. He knew that Chilion was dead, but he still knew that it was not a good thing for the two of them to fall in love and wish to marry. Dedum spoke to Ebenum about his feelings for Orpah. At first, Ebenum denied that he was in love with Orpah, but he soon knew that Dedum was right and he acknowledged to him that he, indeed, loved Orpah. He made a promise to Dedum that he would not have anything to do with Orpah and that he would not again speak to her about anything while they were responsible for getting her to her mother's house. They hugged because they were friends and because they both cared for Orpah's wellbeing.

For the next five days and nights of traveling to the house of Orpah's mother, Ebenum did not come around Orpah at any time during the remainder of the trip. Throughout the day, she wanted to look at Ebenum, but he was always in front of them ensuring that she had a safe trip back to her mother's house. Dedum, now took the place of Ebenum where he walked right behind Orpah on the trip home to her mother. Dedum could see that both of them were very sad, but he knew that this was the best for them and he made sure that they did not come in close contact again for the remainder of the trip. Orpah remembered the songs and chants that Naomi had taught her and Ruth and they brought joy to her heart. The days and nights seemed to go faster once she remembered the songs and the chants and finally she was once again in her mother's house.

Chapter Three

ORPAH ARRIVES AT HER MOTHER'S HOUSE

After the long journey, Orpah, Ebenum and Dedum finally arrived at her mother's house. Her mother, sister and one of her five brothers and several of the servants greeted her. She knew immediately that her father was still upset with her for marrying outside of her kinsmen. He had let her know that he would never bless this marriage when she went to speak to him about her marrying Chilion. She had heard from some of the friends that she would periodically see when she was married that her father was not sad over the death of her husband. Although, he did not say anything about Chilion's death, they could tell that he was not saddened by it. In fact, Orpah had not seen her father at any time while she was married to Chilion. She knew that this was the reason that Naomi said for her to go and return to her mother's house. Her mother had always been there for her even when her father did not want her to see Orpah. Her mother would always find a way to see her and to get messages to her. There were trusted servants in her mother's house that Orpah knew would always be there for her when she needed them.

Seeing that Orpah's father and four of her five brothers did not come to meet her troubled Ebenum very much. As a man, he knew that the men would be the ones that the women depended on when they were troubled. He knew that Orpah's mother was a strong and wise woman, but he knew that the power belonged to the men in the family. He had wondered how Orpah's mother would come to see her and send her messages when she was married to Chilion because he knew that her father did not want her to see Orpah. He finally felt that her father really wanted to be sure that Orpah was doing well so he did not become upset when her mother came to see her and when she sent messages. Ebenum knew that her brother who came out to greet her was the stronger brother in the family and he knew that this brother would be there to protect her at all times. Still, because of his love for Orpah, Ebenum felt that he had to let Orpah's mother know that he really loved her even if they could not be together. He, also, wanted to leave a message advising her to be very careful in her mother's house. He dreaded what could and would happen to her if her family found out that she was worshipping the Lord God of Israel instead of their gods. But, Ebenum knew that he could not say anything about her worshipping God to anyone in her mother's house. He wanted her to know that if she could get a message to those family members of the Land of Judah still in the country of Moab that they would get the message to him. Ebenum knew that Orpah had come to love the family of her husband and that the family of her husband had come to love Orpah. Even now, the people of the land of Judah living in the country of Moab knew that Orpah had returned to her mother's house and they had sent a message that they would always be there for her when she wanted to return to them. Orpah was the type of woman who people enjoyed talking to and with and they loved being around her. Ruth was the woman from the country Moab who longed to be around her mother-in-law. She didn't make friends as easily as Orpah. Thus, the people of the land of Judah were not surprise to hear that Orpah was the one who turned back to return to her own people. They, also, knew that Orpah did not really want to return to her mother's house, but, they knew that Orpah knew in her heart that this would be easier on Naomi if she did not follow her back to the Bethelem- judah. Naomi had sent them a message that Orpah was returning home not because she wanted to in her heart, but she knew that this would be the best thing for Ruth and her mother-in-law. She knew that it was difficult for a single woman on her own and an older single woman with two young single women with her would mean extra trouble. So, she decided to return home and she left Ruth with good advice on how to help the two of them survive when they return to Bethlehem-judah.

Ebenum and Dedum bowed to Orpah's mother and asked if they could give her a package that Naomi had sent with them for her. She excused all from the room and instructed the servants to take Orpah to her quarters and to put her clothes and other belongings away. Ebenum had managed to get close enough to the servant who would bring messages from Orpah's mother to her when she was married to Chilion and he knew that this servant would make sure that Orpah received his message. Ebenum told the servant to let Orpah know that if she needed him at any time for her to get the message to his family from the land of Judah living in the country of Moab and he would promptly come to her. The servant had been very careful when bringing messages to Orpah from her mother. Ebenum knew that only he had seen the servant getting very close to Orpah so that he could tell her what her mother wanted her to know. Chilion had once mentioned to him that this was a trusted servant of Orpah's mother and he was the one that she gave important messages to when she wanted Orpah to know what was going on at home.

After giving the package to Orpah's mother and letting her know what Naomi had told them, Ebenum and Dedum left Orpah at her mother's house. When Dedum walked away, Ebenum decided to say to Orpah's mother what he had earlier told the trusted servant of her mother. Of course, Ebenum did not mention to Dedum about speaking to the trusted servant and Dedum, having seen Ebenum speaking to him, did not mention it either. However, Dedum wanted to say to Ebenum that the trusted servant would tell it to Orpah's mother before he would say anything to Orpah because of his loyalty to the family. He knew that this was true because they would do the same thing in the same situation. He didn't want his friend to be hurt, but he decided to keep these thoughts to himself. Before going back to Bethlehem-judah, they stopped by many of the homes of their family members of the land of Judah living in the country of Moab to see their friends and family members. After they spent the night, they later made their way back to Bethlehem-judah where they told Naomi that Orpah was safely back with her mother.

Chapter Four

ORPAH IS BACK IN HER MOTHER'S HOUSE

Orpah knew that she would long to be with Naomi and Ruth, but she had no idea that she would feel the way she felt once Ebenum and Dedum left her and went back home. All that she ever experienced with her husband's family was constantly on her mind. She prayed to God that these feelings would leave her, but it seemed that she could never shake these many fond memories. Although, she loved thinking and reminiscing, she knew that she had to live under the rules of her blood family since she had moved back home to live with them. She knew Naomi had said for her to go back to her mother's house, but Orpah knew that her father and the men in the family were really the ones in control of the house she was living. She knew that they were in control of the house, although neither her father nor her brothers lived with her mother. With Chilion and his family, Orpah had learned how to let her free spirit show each and every day. She loved to laugh and play with the members of her husband's family. She knew that in her mother's house, she could not show that part of her. Women were not expected to show enjoyment in any area of their life. She was expected to do those things that all the women in the house were expected to do. Wives were expected to be submissive in all means when it came to their husbands. The men of course had several wives and each wife with her children had her own house. The women and children remained out of sight until they were summoned to come out and meet with their father.

In Orpah's family, her brothers and their families lived in the same compound that their father lived. Therefore, she would have an opportunity to see them because they would visit their mother for special activities and on special occasions. Although, Orpah's father had several wives and these wives had children by him, she knew that out of all of his children, she was one of his favorites. He was disappointed when she married Chilion, however, he did not disown her, which is something that he could have done. He could have forbid her from ever coming back to the family's compound, but he did not, thus; she and Naomi knew that he cared about her.

Orpah could hear the little feet of her many nieces, nephews, cousins and other young members of her extended family running outside in the courtyard and down the long halls in her mother's house. She wanted to know what was happening to bring so many of the family members together when no special day or special activities were occurring. She was hoping that no one had come over because she had returned to her mother's house. Orpah did not want to be bothered now, especially when she was feeling so down because she was no longer with those she loved so dearly. She knew that her feelings would show on her face when she was around others and she did not want to cause any problems now since she was living at home again. The door to her living quarters opened and there stood a beautiful young lady who looked so much like her that she gasped before she knew it. Orpah asked the young lady her name and the young lady responded that her name was Sareah and then she said that she knew who Orpah was because they had come over to see her. Orpah remembered that she had a niece named Sareah by the brother who had come to meet her, but she couldn't imagine that Sareah had grown to be such a beautiful young lady. At this point, Orpah's mother came to inquire about her and to request that she come out to see her family who had come over to welcome her back home. Orpah's greatest fear had become a reality and she knew that she would have to come out to see all of the family members who had come to see her. Although, Orpah felt a little sad, yet, at the same time she felt joy in her heart, because she knew now that many family members were glad to see her even if her father did not want to see her.

Orpah put on her favorite garment and made her

face look beautiful, like the beautiful person she was to her family. Her favorite colors were soft blue and white and when she dressed up in these colors Chilion would always say that her true beauty was exposed. So, Orpah felt good for several reasons, she knew that her family was happy that she had returned home and she knew that Chilion was smiling down on her because he loved her wearing beautiful soft blue and white clothes.

When she came into the corridor where her family was assembled, they all smiled and hugged her and the excitement showed throughout the compound. There were melodic music, colorful flowers and an array of foods throughout her mother's house and everyone seemed to enjoy the celebration. Young family members that she did not know existed ran up to her for hugs and kisses and those that she had seen before marrying Chilion had grown and were hardly recognizable. They were glad to tell her their names and who their mother and father were along with the names of their siblings. They brought along gifts that they wanted to give to Orpah and each wanted their gift to be her favorite. Orpah realized that her mother-in-law was so wonderful to send her back home to her family. Naomi knew that her family loved her and she also knew that Orpah loved her family. Orpah danced with all of her young relatives and she wished with all her heart that she had had children with Chilion, but she did not dwell on the negative feelings. She was happy to be back in her mother's house.

Chapter Five

ALL DO NOT WELCOME ORPAH HOME

Although Orpah woke up the morning after her celebration feeling delighted, she could not forget that her father and all of her brothers except one did not show up during the celebration. She knew that this meant that they did not approve of her returning to her mother's house. Orpah prayed to God that this would not be true, because she loved her father and brothers very much. She had wished that they had accepted that she loved Chilion and that she had never wanted to marry one of her family members. In Orpah's culture, young women were expected to marry one of the cousins who would go to the father of the young lady and request his blessings on their marriage. Throughout the days when Orpah was growing up in her mother's house, Orpah would let her cousins know that she did not want to marry one of them. She was not afraid to let them know that she wanted to marry for love and nothing else. Therefore, when she met Chilion and they fell in love, none of her cousins were surprised when they heard that Orpah had married outside of her family. In fact, they had made it clear to their family that they had no desire to marry Orpah.

Orpah resented her father and brothers insisting that she marry someone that they approved instead of allowing her to marry the man that she loved. The men felt that the women and young women in the family did not have a right to refuse an offer of marriage from a family member. Married cousins could also go to the fathers of young women in the family and ask to marry them. The father would request a large sum of money and other expensive items if the married cousin insisted on marrying his young cousin. In most cases, the men would take second and third wives from other families in their tribe. It was uncommon for married cousins to marry young cousins who had never been married. However, if a young cousin's husband had died, they could request to marry her to keep her from living in poverty or to live alone for the rest of her life if her husband had no brothers wishing to marry her.

Orpah, somehow, knew that her father and brothers would continue to insist now, moreso than ever, since Chilion had died that she marries one of the married cousins. She continued to tell her family members that she still desired marrying for love rather than anything else. At her homecoming celebration, she told those who asked that she wanted to marry again for love. She could see the look on her mother's face when she said that she wanted to marry for love, because she knew that her mother wanted her to marry so that she would not be alone for the rest of her life. Her mother had told her many times when she was growing up that women married so that they would not be a burden for their brothers since their brothers have their own families. Orpah knew, although this was not a popular thing for women to proclaim, that she could take care of her own self. She would discuss these things with Chilion and he would tell her to keep these thoughts to herself because men did not like for women to be independent. He would say to her that men want and desire women who are dependent on them for everything in their life. Orpah loved and trusted Chilion and she knew that what he said was the truth, therefore, she never told anyone about her desire to take care of herself.

As time passed, Orpah still had not seen her father or the brothers who did not show up at the homecoming celebration. God had been kind to Orpah since no one in her family had brought up the conversation concerning marriage since her homecoming celebration. She knew what was expected of her when it came to her family and their gods. She never disrespected the gods or the ceremonies associated with the gods. She was in attendance at all celebrations and special observances to the gods. She presented those foods to the gods that her family members and others in the tribe were expected to do and she did her share of the upkeep around the sacred grounds and temples of the gods. Orpah had prayed to the Lord God of Israel to show her what to do while living in her mother's house. God showed her those things that she had to do so that others would not question her sincerity and commitment to their gods. Orpah did not have a problem with the things that she was doing, since she knew that God was in control of her life and He was directing her path every hour and every day. She would pray silently to God and she would thank Him for loving her and for being with her throughout each waking moment. She saved the early morning before dawn when all were sleeping to get on her knees and pray to the Lord God of Israel for His loving kindness in her life. Orpah knew that God had not allowed her father to demand that she marries someone that he had chosen. This, Orpah knew was the grace of God, because God knew that she really loved Chilion more than any other man in her life. But God took Chilion from her and Orpah knew that God had sent Ebenum to replace Chilion in her life. Orpah loves Ebenum like she loved Chilion and she knew that Ebenum loved her too. Orpah also knew that she must do God's Will and wait patiently for Him to bring Ebenum back into her life. Because of His love for her and her love for God, she knew that God would make everything right again in her love life.

Chapter Six

OTHER WORSHIPPERS OF GOD

Live With Orpah

It is the time of the season when the people of the land of Judah living in the country of Moab will travel to the area near the family's compound. She knew that they would be looking for her and she has prayed to God to show her how to get to them because she, too, wanted to see them very much. Orpah knew that this would be a very dangerous time for her since her family is still watching her very closely. Although, they are not asking her about marriage, they are watching the things she's doing and the places she visits throughout the day. Because, Orpah knows that they are still very curious about her devotion to their gods, she has been careful about everything she does around anyone who is in her presence.

The day has arrived when the people of the land of

Judah will pass by the family's compound. Somehow, Orpah's family has always been curious about these people, but, today, they seem exceptionally curious, and this bothers Orpah very much. She knows that her family believes that her husband's family is trying to get her to return to their area, but Orpah knows that this is not true. Her husband's family would do nothing to cause her any harm and they know that these actions would make her father and brothers disown her. Orpah can hear the familiar sounds from the people to let others know that they are traveling into their territory. These sounds are chants of prayers and songs of appreciation that they send up to their God for bringing them on a safe journey into others' territories. Orpah loves these chants and songs and she begins to sing without knowing that she is singing. She soon realizes what she is doing and stops immediately because she knows that others may be listening.

Although, Orpah is alone in her quarters, she hears a sound and quickly turns to see her niece, Sareah, watching her. Sareah starts singing the song that Orpah had been singing just before she realized that she was singing one of the songs that her husband's family sings. She moves closer to Sareah and puts her hand over her mouth to signal her to stop singing this song. She pulls her beautiful young niece to her and whispers that she is never to sing this song in her grandmother's house or around any family members again. She tells her to forget that she has ever heard this song and to never again sing this or any songs that she hears from the people of the land of Judah. Orpah's niece loves her and wants to be like her beautiful aunt. Orpal realizes why her father and brothers were troubled when she came back home. She has finally seen the danger she has brought to her niece by coming back to her mother's house. Now, Orpah wishes that her mother-in-law, Naomi, were here to give her the advice that she needed so badly at this moment. Orpah knows that Naomi is not here and she must make the decisions that she will have to make-to-make things right.

Sareah tells Orpah that she knows all of the songs and chants of her husband's family because she has heard them when Orpah prays in the early mornings to her God. This is the first time Orpah really becomes afraid since she has come back to her mother's house. She wants to know all that Sareah knows and how and when did Sareah hear her chants and songs. Sareah says that she gets up when Orpah gets up and walks to Orpah's quarters making sure that no one sees her. She likes Orpah's God better than the gods of her family because she has prayed to Him and He has helped her in her time of needs. She sees how happy Orpah is when she's praying and singing to her God and she wants to be happy like Orpah. Sareah starts crying and pleads with Orpah to let her know her God like she knows Him. Orpah starts crying with Sareah and hugs Sareah and lets her know that she will tell her about the Lord God of Israel like her husband and his family told her. She cautions Sareah and tells her that no one is to know what she tells her because both of them could be killed if others found out that she was talking to her about the God of the people of the land of Judah.

Orpah knew that her father and mother would miss her so she told Sareah to leave her quarters and to return to her family's quarters. Sareah wanted to stay with Orpah because she was so very happy that Orpah was going to tell her about her God. Sareah was so happy that she wanted Orpah to know that she had seen another person pray to Orpah's God. Orpah wanted to know how Sareah was able to know that someone else was worshipping God, but she knew that Sareah was being missed by her family and she knew that Sareah needed to return to her mother's house right away. Orpah hugged her niece and made sure that no one saw her leave her quarters. She promised Sareah that they would see each other tomorrow, but in the meantime, she made Sareah make a promise not to tell anyone what they had talked about. She knew that Sareah was very close to her younger sister and her father, who is Orpah's oldest brother, and she wanted to be sure that Sareah would not talk to them about anything that had occurred this day.

The day had become a particularly strange and very stressful one for Orpah, but she needed to find out what person in the family's compound was worshipping her God. She knew that this person had to be a strong and courageous individual to be able to worship the Lord God of Israel while others around him or her were worshipping the many gods of the people of her tribe. Never had Orpah suspected that any other person in her family's compound was worshipping the God of the people of the land of Judah. Orpah started thinking and wondering who could be worshipping God without her knowledge. She thought of all the servants who had accompanied her mother when she came to see her or those who brought messages to her from her mother. She thought of the other people in her tribe who worked along side of her when she did her chores around the temples of the many gods and she thought of those who brought foods for the gods. Orpah thought of her many friends who had continued loving her even when she married outside of her kinsmen. Even though she wanted to see her husband's family, she could not stop thinking of what Sareah had told her about having seen this person. Orpah began to wander if her family from the land of Judah knew about this person.

Throughout the day and night, Orpah continued to hear the chants and the songs from her family of the land of Judah. She wanted to see them but she had decided after hearing about this other worshipper of God in the family's compound that this was not the day to see her husband's family. She knew that they would let her know about Naomi and Ruth and she wanted to know if Ebenum had been back to see them since he and Dedum left her mother's house. She had so many things that she wanted to ask her husband's family, but Orpah prayed to God and she knew that this was not the day to see them.

She
began to be concerned about her niece and whether anyone suspected Sareah of not wanting to worship the gods of her family. She knew that she was not too much older than Sareah when she met Chilion and they fell in love and married. Orpah knew that her father and brothers had not forgotten when she fell in love and wanted to marry outside of their kinsmen. She wondered if this was what Sareah was saying when she said that God had helped her when she needed Him the most. So many thoughts were going through Orpah's mind that she could not go to sleep, although she was so very tired. Finally, after saying a prayer to God Orpah went to sleep.

The sweet chants and the lovely songs of her family of the land of Judah woke her up at the usual time that she gets up to pray to God. Orpah felt the desire to walk the path that her niece walks when she sees her praying to God. She wanted so badly to know what other person was praying to God in her family's compound. Orpah wanted the person to know that she knew about him or her and she wanted to talk to them about the goodness of God. It had been so long since she had someone to talk to about the goodness of God. She longed for the days when she talked with Chilion and the days that she talked with Naomi and Ruth. She felt excitement again in her life because she knew that she was not alone in the family's compound. Orpah knew that she would again be with her husband's family and she knew that this person who she doesn't know would leave the family's compound with her. She wanted her niece to go with them, but she did not want to hurt her family and she knew that this would upset the family.

Orpah got dressed and started to open her door, but as she opened the door she saw some of the servants near the door. She immediately closed the door and knew that her father had sent them to guard her so that she would not go and see the people of the land of Judah. This was not what Orpah wanted to do; she wanted to see the other person who was worshipping her God in the family's compound. Although, Orpah could have outsmarted the servants sent to guard her, she did not want to cause harm to this person who she did not know. Orpah wanted to be sure that Sareah had not come to see her this morning, because the servants would see her. She listened very carefully to see if anyone had seen Sareah and she prayed to God for Him to let her know what she needed to do to protect Sareah. She knew that Sareah loved her and wanted to be like her, but Orpah did not want any harm to come to Sareah because of the love and admiration Sareah had for her.

Chapter Seven

ORPAH FINDS THE OTHER WORSHIPPERS OF

Her God

It had been two days since Orpah had heard from her niece, Sareah, and she was becoming very concerned about her safety. She was also concerned whether the other worshipper of her God had found out that Sareah had spoken to her about him or her. There were so many thoughts Orpah were concentrating on that she had literally forgotten about her family of the land of Judah camping out in their city. With her mind solely fixed on Sareah and the other worshipper of God living in her family's compound, neither did she have time to think about the concerns of her father, brothers and other family members. Orpah, however, knew that she had to locate Sareah to find out if someone had learned that the two of them had spoken about Sareah wanting to worship the Lord God of Israel. She could no longer stay in her quarters, simply, because her father had sent servants to watch her every move. More importantly to Orpah now was the wellbeing of her niece and the wellbeing of the worshipper that she did not know. She knew that this person was putting their own existence in danger by staying in a compound where all the inhabitants were expected and commanded to worship the gods of the compound. Orpah knew that she could help protect this person by letting him or her know that God was protecting all of them. She knew that she had to find the two most important people in her life right now and these are Sareah and the unknown worshipper of God.

Orpah decided to leave her quarters in search of these two most important people, Sareah and the worshipper. She did not have any cares or concerns about the servants following her. Orpah knew that she would lose them when she wanted to lose them, because she knew the family's compound like no other person living in this compound. She remembered when growing up with her sister and brothers, whenever she wanted to be alone, Orpah would go to her many hiding places that she alone knew existed in the compound. She knew of hiding places that she had never told others about. She wanted Sareah and the other worshipper of her God to know about these places because they would need to know places to go when they wanted to talk or to be alone with God. Orpah knew that the servants were following her, but she did not want them to know that she knew her father had sent them. She walked at a steady pace watching those around her making sure that no one became overly concerned about her activities.

Orpah knew that the time had come for her to move away from the servants so that she could look diligently for Sareah and she knew that when she finds Sareah, she would then know the name of the unknown worshipper. As Orpah walked faster, she could hear the servants were moving faster and getting closer to her. At this point she knew that she had to move into one of the secret hiding places so that they would pass by her and she could then walk back to the quarters of Sareah's mother. When she passed the corridor earlier that led to Sareah's quarters she saw some strange persons. Orpah wanted to know why these persons would be in her family's compound without her having known about the visitors. Orpah ducked into a strange hole in a wall that others did not know existed. She had been in this hiding place many times when she was growing up in the family's compound. She could still smell the sweet odor of the flowers that she planted years earlier and it seemed that God had not allowed these flowers to grow like the other flowers so that others would not know of this hiding place. Yet, Orpah could see that the flowers were as healthy as the ones on the outside and she knew that this was, again, the goodness of God in her life.

Orpah could hear the servants moving at a fast pace in front of her hiding place. She could hear that they were disgruntled that they had lost her. She could hear them saying that they had to move faster so that they could catch up with her. If they lose her and she goes to her family of the land of Judah, her father would be furious with them and would punish them severely. Although, Orpah did not want them to be severely punish, she could not let them know of her hiding place because God wants her to find Sareah and His other worshipper. After, Orpah felt that it would be safe for her to come out, she moved carefully and walked among those in the corridor moving quickly to where she felt Sareah could be found.

As Orpah approached the place where she felt that Sareah would be, she saw the visitors again speaking with Sareah's mother. Sareah's mother was from Orpah's kinsmen but she was not from one of the families that Orpah had grown up around. Orpah did not know the members of her sister-in-law's family and she had never heard her mother talk about the family. Orpah knew that her eldest brother had married her as his first wife and not one of his cousins as his other brothers had done. She had always been closer to this brother than she was to any of her other brothers. It did not surprise Orpah that this was the brother who had come to welcome her home when she came back with Ebenum and Dedum and she was not surprised that he was at her homecoming celebration. Orpah also knew that this was one of the reasons she loved Sareah like she did. She loved her older brother and would talk to him about anything.

As Orpah reached the house of Sareah's mother she could see her sister-in-law and the visitors turn to look at her. She knew that her sister-in-law had said something to them about her but she did not know what it could have been since she always felt that her sister-in-law cared for her. She was hoping that it was something pleasant and not something that was distasteful. She knew that Sareah's mother loved her gods and would always be obedient to the many gods that she worshipped. This was one of the reasons why Orpah was so concerned about Sareah because she knew that Sareah's mother would be totally against her worshipping the Lord God of Israel. Orpah became troubled again about Sareah's safety now since she has seen her sister-in-law speaking with the strangers. She wonders if these visitors could be from the blood family line of Sareah's mother and if they were then they could harm Sareah if they found out that she did not want to worship their gods. They did not like the God that the people of the land of Judah worshipped and served. She knew that troubling news has brought them to her family's compound. They would never come around the people of the land of Judah because they felt superior over them and did not want to be in their presence. Orpah knew that they were aware that her husband's family was staying near her family's compound.

Orpah cautiously approached her sister-in-law and her guests being especially careful to greet them in a courteous manner. She did not want to alert them that she was searching for Sareah. She asked her sister-in-law if she could see her brother and, immediately, Orpah saw distress in the visitors' face. She did not want anything to happen to her brother and Orpah began to walk into her sister-in-law's quarters. She could see her brother sitting in another room speaking to someone and it seemed that it was a very serious matter that he was discussing with this person. Immediately, Orpah knew that these family members of her sister-in-law were there to ask her brother's permission to marry her niece, Sareah. Orpah knew that Sareah did not want to marry one of her cousins because she had told Orpah that she did not like her cousins on her mother's side. She didn't tell Orpah why she did not like them and now Orpah wished with all of her heart that she had asked her why she didn't like her cousins. She had to speak to her brother on Sareah's behalf to let him know that she did not want to marry one her cousins. As Orpah went into the room where her brother was talking, she could see another person and she could see Sareah sitting very still in the corner of the room. Sareah looked very afraid and seemed to be very unhappy. This bothered Orpah because Sareah had always been a happy person other than when she spoke about her cousins.

The other person in the room that her brother was speaking with did not look like a nice person to Orpah and Orpah knew that she could tell when someone was not a nice person. She had always had a gift of knowing about people and now she knows that God had given this gift to her. When Orpah came into the room, her brother and the visitor stopped speaking and she was glad that they had stopped talking because she knew that they were talking about her niece's future. She apologized for having come over without letting him know that she had wanted to speak to him, but Orpah was very convincing and her brother dismissed the guest from the room and told him that they would talk again at a later time. Orpah could see that her sister-in-law and the other guests were displeased with his decision to terminate the discussion, but they knew that he wanted to talk with his sister. Sareah begged her father to allow her to stay in the room with them because she loved her aunt and wanted to see her. Orpah, also, wanted to see her niece and asked her brother if he would allow her to stay in the room. Before Orpah took a seat, she closed the door behind her to make sure that their conversation was not heard by anyone other than the three of them.

Orpah began the conversation with her brother by letting him know that she loved him and Sareah very much and that she would never do anything to cause any harm to her niece. Orpah told her brother that she knew why the guests had come to their house and the reason was because the cousin wanted to marry Sareah. She told her brother that Sareah had told her that she did not like her cousin and that she did not want to marry any of her cousins. Orpah could sense that her brother was not angry with her for telling him these things. She knew her brother very well and she felt that he agreed with her and he, also, did not want Sareah to marry her cousin. This made Orpah feel confidence in what she was about to discuss with her brother about Sareah desiring to worship the Lord God of Israel instead of worshipping the gods of her family's compound. Orpah moved closer to her brother and motioned for Sareah to move closer to her father so that they could talk about her wish. Orpah knew that if the other family members heard any of the conversation that they would be very upset with the three of them for discussing any other God other than their gods. Orpah made sure that her brother knew that this was the wish of Sareah and that she had not influenced her at all. She did not want to cause any of her family members any problems so she never talked to anyone about the goodness of her God. She remembered what her mother-in-law, Naomi, told her when she talked with her about returning to her mother's house. Naomi told her to always respect her mother's house and not to disrespect her gods. She told her that her mother does not know the goodness of our God and she will not understand your reasons for wanting to worship our God and not the gods that you grew up knowing about. Orpah held her niece's hand and told her brother that Sareah had talked to her in confidence and she had told her niece to keep anything that they had talked bout in complete confidence and not to talk to anyone about their conversation. She went on to tell her brother that Sareah had asked her to talk to her about her God, the Lord God of Israel, because she loves Him more than she loves the many gods that her family members worship. Orpah told her brother that she had cautioned Sareah about the things that could happen to her if anyone found out about her wish to know more about God so that she could worship Him like her aunt worships Him. At that point, Orpah's brother told her that he knew of his daughter's wish and that he, too, wanted to know more about her God because he loves Him more than he loves the many gods that he and his family grew up worshipping. At that moment, it became clear to Orpah that she had finally met the unknown worshipper her niece had told her about. Knowing that her brother is the worshipper of the Lord God of Israel that she wanted to find so badly has made her happier than anything other than finding God for herself.

Chapter Eight

THE WORSHIPPERS OF GOD DEVELOP

A Plan To Leave

The three worshippers of the Lord God of Israel had finally found each other and joy flowed within each of their soul. Orpah had understood the reason Sareah wanted to let her know that she knew of another worshipper of God. She could only talk to Orpah about this because she knew that her father's life would be in danger along with her own life if anyone found out about them. Orpah was glad that they could plan together to leave the family's compound because she knew that they would have to leave if they are to worship God and she knew that they would, indeed, worship the Lord God of Israel until they die. She could tell that her brother and Sareah were determined to leave the family's compound as soon as possible so that they could proclaim their love for God.

Although, the three of them were happy that they could talk to each other about God, they had not forgotten that the problem still existed concerning Sareah and her cousin's marriage proposal. They knew that they had three days left before the visitors would be leaving the family's compound. The cousin has requested that Sareah leaves with them to go back to their family's compound where she would become his bride. Orpah, her brother and Sareah would have to leave the family's compound before the visitors left in three days. Sareah told Orpah that she had seen the servants who accompanied her back to her mother's house give her grandmother a package that Naomi, her mother-in-law, had sent with them. Orpah told both, Sareah and her brother, that she would have to let her mother know what was happening because she felt that her mother would understand and support them. She remembered how her mother and her brother would come and visit her when she lived with Chilion and his family of the land of Judah. She told them that they could go to her husband's family of the land of Judah living in the country of Moab because they had let her know that she could come back whenever she wanted to come. She knew that they would protect and welcome her brother and Sareah and that they would teach them about God like they taught her. Although, Oprah's brother loved his mother and he knew that she would support them in their quest, he cautioned Orpah against telling her their plans, because this would put her in extreme danger with the family. If she did not know what was going on, she could not be questioned as to why she did not tell anyone about their plan. Orpah agreed with her brother because she didn't want anything to happen to her mother because of them. She promised him and Sareah that she would not say anything to her mother about their plan to leave.

Orpah's brother loved his family, but he knew that they would not be able to understand his love for God. He knew that Sareah was the child that was like him more than any of his other children. He was not surprised that she loved the Lord God of Israel like he loved Him. He, also, knew that Sareah's mother would always worship her many gods and would not stay at his family's compound once she finds out that he has left. He knew that she would take Sareah's younger sister and return to her own family's compound. This did not bother him since he felt that she knew that he did not like worshipping the many gods that his family and her family worshipped. Their other children were all married and living with their own families in the compound. Sareah loved her youngest sister, but she knew that they could not take her with them because she did not love God like they loved Him. Sareah and her father agreed that they would not say anything to their family about the decision to leave with Orpah to go live with the people in the country of Moab of the land of Judah. The three of them knew that they would have to

Dr. Catherine J Johnson

devise a plan where no one would be suspicious of them leaving the family's compound forever. Orpah felt joy return to her heart when she thought about returning to her husband's family who loved her like they loved Chilion. Yet, she could not forget the great danger which awaited them when they would actually begin leaving the family's compound. Orpah realized that some of the people of the land of Judah would be leaving going back during the same time that they had to leave the family's compound. She knew that this would be the best way for them to leave, but she had to let her family of the land of Judah know that they wanted to leave as a part of their caravan. Orpah knew in her heart that this was the best way, but she also knew that this was a very danger plan to use, because her father had spies watching her every move. Also, he and the other families in Moab watched everything that the people of the land of Judah did when they were in their territory.

Orpah's brother realized that they had been talking too long and he knew that his wife and her family would soon become suspicious and would want to know what was so important to keep them together for such a long time. He recommended that they get together again tonight because they needed as much time as possible to devise a plan for leaving the family's compound. He knew that they had only two days to develop the plan because they would have to leave during the night so that they would not be noticed by anyone. He, also, knew that they would have to leave the night of the second day because his wife's family members would be leaving during the early morning of the third day to return back to their family's compound. Orpah knew that the plan to leave with the caravan of her husband's family was the best way to leave, but she knew that she would have to convince her brother and Sareah about it when they meet again. Orpah agreed to meet with her brother and Sareah and she told them that the three of them should meet in the corridor to their quarters. She told them that she would then take them to one of her secret hiding places so that others would not know what they were doing. As they were leaving the room, she could see that her sister-in-law and her family members were curious as to what they had discussed in the room for such a long time. They immediately went to Sareah, but she knew not to let them know what the three of them had discussed. Orpah knew that Sareah could be trusted to keep the information to herself.

Chapter Nine

THEY DECIDE ON THE PLAN

As the night approached, Orpah became tensed about the meeting that she had to attend with her brother and Sareah. She wanted very much to tell her mother about their plan to leave the family's compound and more importantly, their reason for leaving. She, somehow, knew that her mother would understand their reason to want to worship the Lord God of Israel, the God that the three of them loved. She knew that her mother understood that she would never be able to worship their family's gods any longer. Her mother had never said anything bad about her worshipping her God and Orpah knew that this was because her mother had accepted the fact that she loved God more than she loved the many gods that her family worshipped. While thinking about her mother, Orpah thought about the package that Sareah had seen Ebenum and Dedum give to her mother from Naomi. She knew that by not talking to her mother about their plan to leave, that she would never know what was in the package. She knew that it would be a very long time before she could see her mother because her father and the other family members would forbid her from contacting Orpah this time. Unlike the first time when she left because she married Chilion, this time she is leaving because she does not want to worship their gods and two other family members are leaving with her to worship her God.

Although thinking about leaving her mother caused her some unhappiness, Orpah knew that she had to leave so that she, her brother and Sareah could be happy and content for the rest of their lives. Orpah realized that it was now dark enough for her to move out of her quarters and move to the corridor of her brother's quarters so that she could take them to the secret hiding place where their meeting would take place. As Orpah left her quarters, she could see that her father's servants were still watching her so she made sure that she was aware of their every move. She knew that they would make sure that they did not lose her this time. They would stay very close to her because they knew she was aware of them and she knew they were there to make sure she did not go to see her husband's family. In fact, Orpah approached them and spoke to each of them because she knew them personally. These were people she had grown up around and she knew them and she knew their families. As she walked off after speaking to each of them, she could tell that they were very close to her and watching her every move. As Orpah reached the corridor to her brother's quarters, she could tell both he and Sareah were concerned and seemed a little agitated. Orpah continued to be calm even though she wanted to know what had agitated her brother and Sareah in such a manner that both of them seemed tensed and agitated. As she approached them, she could tell they had seen the servants who were following her. The three of them hugged and kissed each other so that the servants would not become alarm at their meeting in the corridor. Her brother went to the servants and spoke to them. He had grown up with them and they knew each others and they trusted her brother. Orpah could see that the servants left them after he spoke with them.

When her brother returned to them, he suggested they move quickly to the secret hiding place. He told Orpah and Sareah that he told the servants that he knew his father had them to follow Orpah and he told them to leave and come back later in the night. He told them that he would make sure Orpah did not leave her family's compound to go and see her husband's family. Orpah's brother knew they would return shortly because they were trusted servants of their father and they would do exactly as he directed them. He did not want the servants to become alarm concerning their meeting and to speak to their father about them meeting in the corridor. At her brother's urging, Orpah immediately started them moving in the direction of the secret hiding place. She wanted to know why both her brother and Sareah were agitated, but she wanted to make it to the secret hiding place without losing any more time. She knew they had a lot to talk about concerning the plan they would use to leave their family's compound.

At last, Orpah could see the concealed opening that she had used so many times to go into this favorite hiding place when she was growing up in the family's compound. She had not been back to this hiding place since she had come back to her mother's house and she wanted badly for the three of them to be able to use this opening to get into her secret place. Before they knew it, Orpah's brother and Sareah were inside a place that they had never seen before. They wondered how Orpah knew of such a place and then her brother told Sareah that her aunt, Orpah, was the one in the family who would fantasize and tell them about places they never thought existed. He said that this was one of the places Orpah would tell them about. Although, Orpah enjoyed listening to her brother talk about her, she wanted at this time to know what was troubling both he and Sareah. Her brother said that they had found out after Orpah left them today, that her wife's cousins would be leaving a day earlier than expected and they intended to take Sareah back with them. He said Sareah's mother had promised them she would get him to go along with her wish to let Sareah return to her family's compound so that they could get married. Her brother knew Sareah could not return with her cousins and he knew that

Orpah Walked Ahead of Ruth

they had to make sure their plan was developed tonight because of the news they had heard today. Orpah knew that this was distressing news, but she told her brother and Sareah that God would make sure they leave their family's compound before his wife's cousins left to go back home. Orpah began to tell them about the plan to leave with her husband's family when they return back to their camp. She knew they did not all leave at the same time. She knew that some had already left to go back and some would be leaving to go back the night when they would have to leave their family's compound.

Orpah suggested to her brother that it would be best for him to leave in the early morning to meet with her husband's family to alert them that the three of them would be accompanying them to their home. She told him that he would have to be the one to go to see them because various family members were watching her and Sareah. She told him that she had brought some clothing back with her that the people of the land of Judah are wearing while they are in their territory. She has hid these clothing in a secret place in her quarters so that no one would find them and question her about them. She knew now that this was the reason she had brought the garments back so that they would be dressed like them when they went back to their home in the country of Moab. She told her brother that he would have to go to her quarters to get clothing for him and Sareah to wear when they left the compound. He also would have to have clothing on like the people of the land of Judah when he goes to meet with them to take them her message. She knew he would have to conceal these items until he gets close enough to her husband's family. When he gets close enough and he is sure that their family members and others in their tribe were not watching him, he would then put on the clothing that Orpah gave him so that her husband's family would welcome him into their camp.

Her brother agreed that he would be the one to go the camp of her husband's family in the very early morning before dawn. He knew that this would be the best time to go so that others would not see him leaving and going to the camp of the people of the land of Judah. Although, they were not camping that far from their family's compound, he knew that it would take him some time to get to them because of the danger involved in getting to them. Fortunately, he knew where people from his tribe, who were watching the activities of the people of the land of Judah, would be stationed during the night and early morning. Her brother knew that he would take an alternate route to get to their camp, but this would take more time than usual and they needed every minute in the day to make sure their plan to leave the family's compound was realized. Orpah and her brother left Sareah at her mother's quarters and he accompanied Orpah back to her quarters so that she could give him the items that he needed. While walking back to her quarters, they met the trusted servants of their father who had been sent to spy on Orpah. They were returning back to the corridor and Orpah's brother told them that she had wanted to return earlier and that he decided to walk her back. They told him that he could go back home because they would walk her the rest of the way, but Orpah's brother told them that he wanted to see his mother and he continued walking with them. When they reached her quarters, the servants stayed on the outside while Orpah and her brother went into her quarters. She gave him the clothing and they promised to meet ready to leave their family's compound around midnight. They decided to meet where Sareah had seen Orpah praying in the early mornings, because her brother felt that this was the safest place to meet, since his wife's cousins were still with them and would be rising shortly afterward to return to their family's compound.

When leaving his sister's quarters, Orpah's brother decided to move out of his family's compound to go and take the message to the family of Orpah's husband. He felt that his father's servants were becoming suspicious and he did not want them to follow him back to his quarters. He left in a direction that put him closer to the camp of the people of the land of Judah. He was able to slip on the garment that Orpah had given him to wear when he met with her husband's family and he put his regular clothing on top of this garment. He put the clothing for Sareah under his top so that no one would see him carrying something when he left his sister's quarters. He knew that the servants were smart and would tell his father if he took anything from Sareah's room when he left her quarters. As he passed the places where his tribesmen were watching the activities of the people of the land of Judah, he could see that some were asleep and did not see him pass by them. This was good news, he knew that he had to move very fast so that these same persons would be on duty when he returned from the meeting place.

Things were going very well and he knew that he was not far from the camp of the people of the land of Judah. Before he realized it, several persons had surrounded him and he was afraid because he did not know these people. He started to explain, but he was pushed by several of the men in the direction of a large tent. Here, he saw many of the elders of the people of the land of Judah sitting around in a large circle chanting to the Lord God of Israel. He knew that he had to obey those who had pushed him into this tent and he kept all thoughts to himself. Orpah's brother scanned the room to see if he could remember seeing any of these people when he came with his mother to visit Orpah and Chilion. At one point, his eye focused on an older man who he thought was related to Naomi's husband, Elimelech, and surely enough, the elder gentleman smiled back at him. This made his heart glad, because he knew that there was someone here who knew him and would speak well about his motives for coming to their camp. The elder gentleman arose and went to Orpah's brother to inquire why he had been captured around their camp. He swiftly told him that he was bringing a message from Orpah to them to let them know that Orpah, his daughter and

Orpah Walked Ahead of Ruth

he would be going back to live with them in their home territory in the country of Moab. He explained to him that he and his daughter, like Orpah, loved their God and wanted to serve and worship Him, rather than the gods of his family. He, also, told him that he had worn clothing like they had on so that he would be invited to come in and talk with them. He explained that before he could remove his top clothing that was covering the garment that Orpah gave him to wear when meeting them; the people of the land of Judah sited him. The elder gentleman left to speak with his people about what Orpah's brother had told him.

When the elder gentleman had finished speaking with the men in the room, one of the leaders in the circle came up to Orpah's brother and asked him to remove his top clothing so that they could see the garment that Orpah had given him to wear when meeting with them. When her brother removed his top clothing and the men saw the garment that he was wearing had belonged to Chilion, they immediately accepted him in their circle by embracing him. They let Orpah's brother explain what had been happening to her and why he had taken such a dangerous chance to meet them while people from his tribe were watching them closely.

After the men in the tent heard of the situation that the three of them were facing they told Orpah's brother that he and Sareah were welcomed to go back with them. The men told him that they would always welcome him and his daughter because they love and accept Orpah in their family, because she was Chilion's wife and she is the daughter-in-law of their own Elimelech and Naomi.

Chapter Ten

THE WORSHIPPERS TRAVEL TO

A New Home

After the men in the tent heard the story and received the message that Orpah had sent with her brother, they let two of the men in the camp accompany Orpah's brother back to his family's compound. They knew of a route that would get him back home quicker than the route that he had taken to get to them. This route was one that he and the others in his tribe did not know existed. In a very short time, Orpah's brother found himself back at his family's compound. He realized that the men had brought him back so that he, Orpah and Sareah could use this route when they leave to travel to their new home.

As they planned, the three of them met at the place where Sareah would see Orpah praying in the early mornings. Orpah, her brother and Sareah were excited, but at the same time a little sad about leaving their family members, yet, they knew in their heart that this was the thing that they had to do. None of them spoke about their feelings, they hugged and cried and began the journey to their new home. Orpah's brother told them about the new route that he learned of today and he told them that he knew that this was the way that they should take to leave to meet the people of the land of Judah. Orpah and Sareah followed him out of the family's compound and shortly after leaving the compound, they pulled their top clothing off and her brother buried the garments in a small hole near a large tree. Immediately, after burying the clothes, they proceeded to the campsite of their new family. They found that the men, women and children were waiting for them and that they were excited that they had decided to join them. Orpah was so happy to see the family of her husband, the people that she had come to love so much. Their new family decided to separate the three of them so that they would not be together when they are walking back to their territory located in the country of Moab. The people of the land of Judah felt that if people from their tribe came looking for them that it would be harder to spot them if they were separated from each other. This pleased the three of them and they hugged each other and went to the place where their new family wanted them to be when they journeyed back to their new home.

Orpah knew that the time had come for them to leave with the group that would be going back to their territory because of the familiar songs and chants that she heard

Orpah Walked Ahead of Ruth

from the family members. She had heard these songs and chants so often when she lived with Chilion, and after his death, when she lived with Naomi and Ruth. Orpah loved these songs and chants and she wanted so badly to sing them with her brother and Sareah. But, she knew that they knew the songs and chants because she had heard them sing the songs and say the chants when they told her that they wanted to worship her God. She listened carefully so that she could hear them among the people and surely enough, she could hear her brother and Sareah singing and chanting with their new family. The family members began to move away from the place where her family's compound was and Orpah felt sad that she had not spoken with her mother about them leaving to go back with the people of the land of Judah. She knew that her mother would be happy for the three of them because her mother wanted her children to be happy. But as she started to shed a tear, she thought of her mother being questioned by her father and the other men in their tribe and Orpah knew immediately that she had done the right thing when she did not speak with her mother about them leaving the compound. She prayed to God that her mother would understand why they left and would be all right with the three of them leaving the family's compound so that they could serve and worship the Lord God of Israel. Calmness came upon Orpah and she knew that God had fulfilled the prayer that she had prayed. She knew that her mother was fine with them leaving with her husband's family. She began to sing the songs and she began to say the beautiful chants that Chilion and Naomi had taught her.

As the midday sun pounded upon his head, Orpah's brother realized that his wife's cousins had left his family's compound and he was sure that his wife and their youngest daughter had gone back with them. He reasoned that by this time, those searching for them would have come upon them if they were still searching for them. He presumed that the cousin who wanted to marry Sareah did not want to look for her because he knew that she had left so that she could worship her aunt's God. Those in the family knew that he and Sareah had left with Orpah and this meant that they wanted to serve the God that Orpah served and not the many gods that their family and the people of their tribe served. He loved his family, but he knew that he could never love the gods of his family like he loved the Lord God of Israel. Thus, he knew that he and Sareah would fare much better in life by leaving their family's compound and going with Orpah to live with the family of Chilion and Naomi. Orpah's brother knew that Naomi loved Orpah like she was her own daughter and he knew that if they had to leave the country of Moab and go to Bethlehem-judah that she would take him and Sareah in as her family. He knew that they, like Ruth, were not of the land of Judah, but he had heard from some of the people of the land of Judah that Ruth and Naomi were doing very well in Bethlehem-judah.

Finally, Orpah could see the beautiful landscape of

Orpah Walked Ahead of Ruth

the community that she loved so much those wonderful years she was with her husband and later when she stayed with her mother-in-law. She wanted to be able to tell Sareah the great things that she would be able to see and do in this community that she will call her new home. Orpah looked around through the many family members to see if she could see her brother or Sareah, but there were so many people that she could not see either at this time. Those who had made it back to their territory came out to meet the large group that was coming back. Orpah could see so many people that she had called her family for such a long time, but it had been a long time since she had seen them and she wondered if they would still recognize her. Those who started coming out to meet them had already received the news that she, her brother and Sareah were coming back to make their territory their home. She was happy to hear them say her name and many of them asked about her brother and Sareah. Orpah could see some of the men in the family bringing her brother and Sareah to her and this made her heart jump for joy that the two of them were still with her. She could see that her brother and Sareah were just as happy as she was to see that she was still with them. The three of them were taken to the house that they would live in and this home belonged to Elimelech and Naomi. They were the family of Elimelech and Naomi and therefore the house belonged to them now. This made Orpah extremely happy because when she had been married to Chilion, she lived in this house with her father-in-law and mother-in-law.   Orpah knew now that she, her brother and Sareah would be very happy because they would live together in the home of her husband's family.

Chapter Eleven

SAREAH KEEPS A SECRET

Orpah, her brother and Sareah found out that the servants that had been with Elimelech and Naomi before Naomi left to go back to the Bethlehen-judah would become their servants now. They had gone to live with other families when Naomi left, but they now wanted to come back to their master's house and live with Orpah, her brother and Sareah. Orpah was glad to see the ones that did not leave with Naomi come back to be with them and she knew that Naomi would be glad that they had come back to their home. But, Orpah somehow knew that Naomi already was aware that the servants had come back to be with them. Naomi was that type of a woman and a mother-in-law. She would rather have the servants' stay with Orpah, her brother and Sareah to make sure that they had the things that they needed rather than have them move to Bethlehem-judah to be with Ruth and her. Orpah knew that her mother-in-law had left some of her servants in the country of Moab to be there when she would come back to her husband's family. She felt that Naomi always knew that one day she would return to their territory in the country of Moab.

Orpah could see that her brother and Sareah were fitting in very well with their new family and her brother was quickly becoming one of the leaders in his new community. They were attending all classes, ceremonies and any activities that taught them more about the Lord God of Israel. Orpah wanted Naomi and Ruth to know that her brother and Sareah were very happy to be with the people of the land of Judah. She had learned of the wonderful things that Naomi and Ruth were doing and she would send messages whenever someone would leave to go back to Bethlehem-judah. But, she wanted to tell them herself and to let them see how happy they were and how quickly they were being accepted and loved by their new family. She would hear from Naomi and Ruth many times during the month because they would send her messages by anyone coming and leaving. But, Orpah wanted to see them herself and she knew that one day soon she would see Naomi and Ruth. Orpah began making plans for the three of them to visit Naomi and Ruth in Bethlehem- judah.

Orpah wanted to hear about the things that her brother and Sareah were involved in and she decided to have a small celebration so that all of their new friends could come to their new home. During their evening meal, she decided to tell them about the celebration that

Orpah Walked Ahead of Ruth

she was planning for them so that they could invite their new friends to their new home. This seemed to make her brother and Sareah happy that their new found friends would be able to come to their home. While, Orpah was generating ideas for the party, Sareah stopped her from talking and asked that she and Orpah's brother, her father, listen to her because she needed to talk with them about something very important that had been bothering her since she came to her new home. Of course, this brought great concern to Orpah, because she wanted to be sure that all had been well with Sareath and her brother since they had come to live with her husband's family. Orpah could not think of anyone bothering Sareah or her brother and she was anxious to find out what had been bothering Sareah since she came to their new home.

Orpah and her brother could see that Sareah was having problems talking about this subject that was causing her much concern. Sareah's father asked her if it would be easier for her to talk if he left the room, but Sareah said that she needed to speak to both of them. Orpah moved closer to her niece and took her hand to let her know that everything was all right. She told Sareah to speak freely because they were family and whatever was bothering her should be shared with her father and her. When Orpah spoke to Sareah, things seemed to become clearer and Sareah felt she could share this deep secret she had been carrying with her since she left their family's compound with the two people she loved the most in her life, except for her grandmother. Sareah loved her grandmother more than she loved her mother or her father. Sareah started to tell them the secret. She told them that she did not want them to distrust her and she did not want them to be upset with her because she had done something that the three of them had agreed that they would not do. Sareah said that she had gone to see her grandmother before they left their family's compound because she couldn't make herself leave without seeing her precious grandmother before leaving her forever. She didn't think that her grandfather would allow her grandmother to visit them like he had allowed her to visit Orpah when she was married to Chilion. Sareah told them that she had prayed to God and He had assured her through the wonderful feelings that fell upon her that things would be all right if she went to see her grandmother before leaving to go and live with the people of the land of Judah. Orpah and her brother were interested in knowing the rest of Sareah's story and they both spoke at the same time asking Sareah to go on and tell them what had happened when she saw her grandmother. Sareah said to them that she had hugged her grandmother and she told her that the three of them were leaving the family's compound during the night to go and meet with the family of Orpah's husband. She told her grandmother that they were leaving forever to go and live with the people of the land of Judah and like the people of the land of Judah they were going to worship the Lord God of Israel. Sareah told them that she had

Orpah Walked Ahead of Ruth

told her grandmother that she and her father had grown to love the Lord God of Israel with all of their heart and they knew that they would never be able to worship and serve the gods of their family ever again. Sareah told them that her grandmother already knew that she and her father did not want to serve and worship their gods any longer. Her grandmother told her that she was happy that they had found the God that they wanted to worship and serve from now on. Sareah said that her grandmother called her into another room and gave her a package to give to Orpah, but because of her disloyal to them, she had been hiding the package since they left the family's compound. She pulled the package from a bag that she had slipped under the chair she was sitting in at the table. She handed the package to Orpah and said her grandmother wanted Orpah to have the package when they moved into their new home. Sareah said she thought that this was the package Naomi had given to Ebenum and Dedum to give to Orpah's mother. Orpah took the package and thanked her niece for having the courage to go and see her grandmother before she left the family's compound. She and her brother said to Sareah that they would never distrust her when she did what God had wanted her to do and they were sure that the Lord God of Israel was directing her path.

The three of them hugged each other and Orpah and her brother reassured Sareah that she had done what God wanted her to do when she told her grandmother that they were leaving and especially when she explained why

Dr. Catherine J Johnson

they chose to leave the family's compound. Sareah said to them that she felt much better now that they knew what she had been keeping to herself since they left their family. She said that she had been having a hard time going to sleep at night and that many times during the night she would awake and feel sad that she had spoken to her grandmother when they had agreed not to talk to her about the decision to leave. Orpah said that since they were tired and the three of them wanted to go to their room, she suggested that they continue the conversation about the celebration tomorrow evening. They all agreed to bring suggestions to help make the celebration a fun party for them and their friends. The three of them left for their room to retire for the evening.

Before Orpah could retire to her room, Sareah ran up to her and said that she wanted to say something else to her in confidence. She did not want her father to hear this conversation because she felt that her father may not approve of what she was going to say to Orpah. When Sareah would usually speak to Orpah about any matter which pertained to Orpah alone, she would in most cases, let her father know what she wanted o talk to Orpah about. But, in this case, she didn't want her father to know about this subject. Orpah invited Sareah to come into her room so that they could speak in private, so that her father would not become suspicious if he saw them speaking outside of her room. Sareah said that her grandmother had also sent another message by her to give to Orpah. She said that when her grandmother gave the package to her, she smiled a little and said that she was going to say this to Orpah, but since she was leaving to be happy, she wanted Sareah to give her another message when she gave her the package. Orpah, at this point, was about to shout at Sareah to tell her what her mother had said because she wanted to know what made her grandmother smile when she was talking to her. But, Orpah knew that this would only make her brother and the servants want to know what had caused her to shout at this time of the night. So, Orpah remained calm and waited to hear the other message that her mother had sent by Sareah. Sareah was a little hesitant because she did not know how her aunt felt about a servant being in love with her. At this point, Orpah told Sareah that she was anxious to hear the message that her mother had sent by her to give to her. Sareah said that her grandmother had told her to tell her that one of the servants that accompanied her back home wanted her to let her daughter know that he cared for her a lot. In fact, Sareah said that her grandmother felt that Ebenum was in love with her daughter. Her grandmother said that he wanted to be sure that things would be all right for Orpah since she had decided to come back to her house. He had told her that if Orpah ever wanted to return to the people of the land of Judah's territory that all she had to do was to get a message to any of the family members and that he would make sure that she would be able to come back and live a wonderful life. She said the reason her grandmother felt that Ebenum was in love with her was because he never mentioned her mother-in-law, Naomi, being the one concerned about her wellbeing. Her grandmother told her that she was sure her mother-in-law, Naomi, was concerned and would be happy to hear that she wanted to come back, but Ebenum made sure she knew that these were his feelings concerning her daughter.

This made Orpah very happy and Sareah could see that her grandmother had sent the message because she knew this would bring happiness to Orpah. Sareah could see that Orpah was in love with Ebenum and was so very happy that she had brought this message to her from. Orpah told Sareah to keep this little secret to herself until she told her brother about Ebenum being in love with her. She could see that Sareah wanted to know how she felt about Ebenum and Orpah told her niece that she loved Ebenum like she loved Chilion. She said that they had not talked about their feelings for each other, but she was sure that Ebenum loved her like she loved him. Orpah told Sareah that when they were accompanying her back home, he was such a caring person. He would always do something special to make sure that the journey back was comfortable for her. Although, he did not speak to her, she could see in his eyes that he loved her very much. Orpah said that she could tell even when Chilion was living that Ebenum liked her better than he liked Ruth and that Dedum cared for Ruth more than he cared for her. Sareah was so happy to hear that her aunt was in love again and she wanted to know when she would let

Ebenum know that she was back with their family of the land of Judah.

Although Orpah had not heard from Ebenum, she knew in her heart that he had heard they had come to live with the people of the land of Judah. She told Sareah that Naomi sent her a message telling her that Ruth had married a well to do kinsman of Elimelech. She said that this kinsman of Elimelech had let the two devoted servants, Ebenum and Dedum, become landowners themselves and they were no longer servants. Naomi, also, told her the kinsman that Ruth married gave the house that belonged to Elimelech that the three of them lived in to them. When he purchased the parcel owned by Elimelech that meant the house in the country of Moab belonged to him. When Ruth told him about the three of them coming to live with the people of the land of Judah, her husband gave the house to them. This made Sareah happy and she wanted to share this news with her father because she knew he wanted to hear the good news that her aunt had shared with her this night. But, Sareah remembered her promise to her aunt. She asked her aunt to tell her more about Ebenum. Orpah told her that Naomi had sent a message concerning both, Ebenum and Dedum. She told her that Naomi had said that after the two of them became landowners, Dedum stayed around her to make sure she would be all right, but Ebenum was doing very well as a landowner away from them. She said she felt Naomi knew in her heart that Ebenum loved her and she was pleased about it.

Orpah told Sareah that Naomi believed Ebenum would be coming back to live with his family in the country of Moab one day. Orpah could see that Sareah was very happy about hearing all the news she had shared with her and Orpah knew Sareah wanted to tell her father about the good news. Orpah told Sareah that she could share the good news with her father because she could see that she wanted badly to tell him about the things that she had heard this night. Sareah said that she was so happy she had told her that she did not have to keep the news she heard tonight a secret. She did not want her aunt to be upset with her so she had decided she could not tell her father what they had talked about. Sareah said that she was sure her father would be as happy as she was to hear the good news about his sister being in love again. Orpah could see that Sareah wanted to stay all night to hear more about Ebenum, but she told her that she had to go to bed because it had gotten late and both of them had to get up early to do their chores.

Chapter Twelve

GOD BLESSED HIS WORSHIPPERS

When Orpah woke up the next morning from a restful sleep, she could hear
the voices of her brother and Sareah. She knew that they were having a pleasant conversation because each of them was laughing throughout the conversation. She also knew when her brother became excited about something, his voice would become ecstatic in nature and he would literally be shouting out his words. This was exactly what her brother was doing this morning as he and Sareah were talking. Orpah knew that Sareah had told her father about the things they talked about last night and she could tell that he was extremely happy.

As Orpah walked into the room, her brother could not contain his emotions, he ran up to her and grabbed her and began dancing throughout the room. Sareah was so happy that she began dancing along with them and the three danced until they could no longer dance due to exhaustion. Her brother wanted to hear all the things that she had told Sareah last night. He said that Sareal had told him so many things, but he wanted to hear everything from Orpah. While the three of them ate breakfast, Orpah told her brother the things that she had said to Sareah. She talked about being in love with Ebenum and how she felt that he loved her as much as she loved him. She said that she knew they would one day see each other and that God would let them marry as he had let her marry Chilion. Orpah told her brother and Sareah that she had dreamt that one day she and Ebenum would have children together and she knew that God would bless this union. She talked about the house that they live in now belonging to them because the kinsman of Elimelech who married Ruth gave them the house so that they would have their own home in the country of Moab. Orpah's brother, having been a landowner, was delighted to hear this because he wanted very badly to have his own home so his sister and his daughter would have a family compound of their own. Her brother, also, knew that having his own land would enable him to become a leader in his new family and this was something he had prayed to God for since moving home with the people of Judah.

Orpah knew that her brother and Sareah had their own dreams and she wanted them to pursue their dreams as she had pursued her dreams. She knew that the Lord God of Israel was directing and guiding them each day that they walked on His great earth. Orpah was happy that these things had happened to them because she knew they were going to be happy and that they would thrive because of the things that they had experienced. When the three of them finished talking about all that had been discussed by Orpah, they went happily in separate ways to do their chores in the community.

When Orpah, her brother and Sareah had come to the territory of the people of Judah living in the country of Moab, it was still warm during the day and it was very pleasant during the evening, but the season was changing where the air was getting cold during the daylight and the evenings were spent, primarily, at home with immediate families due to the extreme cold weather. During these cold nights, Orpah would find herself in her room thinking about her family that she left in Moab and especially her mother that she loved so dearly. She would also think about Naomi and Ruth back in Bethlehem-judah. But, more than anyone, she would find herself thinking about Ebenum and wondering why Ebenum had not come to be with them in the country of Moab. In her heart, she knew that Ebenum loved her, but she began wondering if Ebenum had married someone else since becoming a landowner. These thoughts caused great pain for Orpah and she knew that thinking thoughts like these would cause her to doubt her God and this was something that she had promised herself that she would never doubt the Lord God of Israel. She would pray each day that these negative and bad thoughts be removed from her mind and surely enough, one night, Orpah did not think of

Ebenum in this manner, she knew that one day soon, she would see Ebenum and they would be together.

Before long, the season was changing and the sun was bringing warm temperatures again to their territory. Orpah's brother had grown and was greatly appreciated by the people of the land of Judah living in the country of Moab. He had been appointed one of the new elders in the community and he was selected to study ways of strengthening ties with those in the country of Moab who did not worship and serve the Lord God of Israel. Sareah had grown to be even lovelier than the time Orpah saw her when she came back to her mother's house. She was a very friendly and respected young lady and many of the young single men in their territory were smitten with love over her unique beauty and the way she carried herself. Sareah had become one of the most popular young ladies in the community. The older women would single her out to teach the ritual and ceremonial traditions that others had taught them when they were her age. She was one of the young ladies that were responsible for preparing specific activities for the boys and girls. Because Sareah was such a caring and compassionate young lady, the children she taught adored her and looked forward to her teaching them the activities.

Orpah's brother knew that when the Lord God of Israel would provide him his bride, that he would marry one of the ladies in his new community, but he was now concerned about his sister and her happiness. He decided to send a message to Ebenum letting him know that he knew of the love that he and his sister shared for each other and that he was happy for both of them. Her brother had heard from some of Ebenum's family living in the territory that he was a prosperous landowner in Bethlehem-judah. He found out that Ebenum had never married because he loved a woman of the people of Judah living in the country of Moab. Orpah's brother did not ask them about the woman because he knew in his heart that the woman was his sister, Orpah. After he sent the message to Ebenum by one of the men who left to visit family members in Bethlehem-judah, her brother waited to hear from Ebenum. Shortly, after his friend had left for Bethlehem-judah, one of the servants of Ebenum brought a message to Orpah's brother. Ebenum sent a message that he and his whole household would be moving to the territory of the people of Judah living in the country of Moab in the very near future. He wanted to thank Orpah's brother for sending him the message and he said that he loved Orpah with all his heart and he wanted to marry her.

Once again, the season was changing and the temperature was becoming cooler during the day and evening. Although Orpah's brother had not heard from Ebenum since he sent him the message, he knew that the Lord God of Israel would let Ebenum come to their territory. Her brother knew that his sister would be extremely happy to see Ebenum and he knew that Orpah thought of Ebenum each day, but he kept it a secret that he had sent Ebenum a message. When the three of them were resting on a cool evening in their rooms, they heard a knock at the door. Orpah did not get up to see who was visiting them since she knew that her brother was well sought after for opinions by others in the community. She presumed that someone needed some advice from him and that they had come over during the evening when they could talk when others would not be present. Sareah had come out of her room and she saw this distinguished looking gentleman talking to her brother. Although, it had been a while since Sareah had last seen Ebenum, she knew immediately that the handsome man was Ebenum and that he had come to see her aunt. She was so very happy for Orpah and ran into her room before asking her father if she could let her aunt know that she had a visitor. When Orpah saw the look on Sareah's face, she wanted to know what had made her so happy, but Sareah told her that she needed to see who her father was speaking with in the corridor. When Orpah came into the corridor, her eyes met the eyes of Ebenum and she knew immediately that he loved her even more than she imagined him loving her and he knew that she loved him just as much as he loved her.

Orpah's brother and his daughter excused themselves from the room so that Orpah and Ebenum could talk about all the things that they had wanted to say when they would see each other again. Orpah and Ebenum were happy to see each other and they talked throughout the night about all the things that had happened to them since they saw each other last. Ebenum told her that he had moved his home from Bethlehem-judah to their territory and that he was having a house constructed where they would live. When he was talking about the house, Ebenum realized that he had not asked her to be his bride and immediately he fell on his knees with tears in his eyes and he asked her to marry him. Orpah said she loved him with all of her heart and that she would love to be his bride. They were very happy and they both got on their knees and thanked the Lord God of Israel for bringing them together again.

About the Author

Catherine Johnson is a resident of Fairburn, Georgia. She grew up in Memphis, Tennessee, where she graduated from Hamilton High School in 1967 and LeMoyne-Owen College with a Bachelor of Science Degree in Elementary Education in 1971. She is a member of Delta Sigma Theta Sorority. She is a member of Christian Fellowship Baptist Church in College Park, Georgia. She also holds a Masters of Science Degree in Instructional Materials from Southern Illinois University, Carbondale, Illinois and a Doctorate of Education from Nova Southeastern University, Ft. Lauderdale, Florida. She is a media specialist at Frederick Douglass High School in Atlanta, Georgia. Catherine married her college sweetheart and they are the parents of three grown children. She is also the author of "Queen Vashti – Beloved Black Queen"

Printed in the United States
92249LV00001B/64-162/A